EGMONT

We bring stories to life

Book Band: Green

First published in Great Britain 2005
This Reading Ladder edition published 2016
by Egmont UK Limited
The Yellow Building, 1 Nicholas Road, London W11 4AN
Text copyright © Tony Bradman 2005
Illustrations copyright © Emma Carlow 2005
The author and illustrator have asserted their moral rights
ISBN 978 1 4052 8225 3
www.egmont.co.uk
A CIP catalogue record for this title is available from the British Library.
Printed in Singapore
42526/15

Series consultant: Nikki Gamble

MIX
Paper
FSC FSC® C018306

Cat Trouble

Feeling Bad

Making
Friends

Cat Trouble

Mum was taking Flora the Fairy to

Nana and Grandpop's house.

Flora didn't want to go.

I'll be late!

Nana and Grandpop were going to look after her while Mum went shopping.

Here we are!

Flora loved them . . . but they had

a cat called Rufus.

And Flora was scared of him.

Flora didn't like the way Rufus
walked softly and silently.

She didn't like the way he followed
her around.

And she didn't like the way he
stared at her with his big scary
green eyes.

Mum knocked on the door, and

Nana opened it.

Where's
Rufus?

See you later!

Rufus didn't seem to be around, so Flora went in. Mum kissed her and flew off.

Nana took Flora into the kitchen.

She sat at the table and did some drawing.

Behind her the cat flap opened slowly . . .

Flora turned round – and there was

Rufus, creeping up on her!

He was staring at her with his big

scary green eyes.

Flora screamed.

'What's going on?'

said Grandpop. They tried

to calm Flora down.

But it was no use.

Oh dear!

Feeling Bad

'Please put Rufus outside again!'
Flora said. So Grandpop did what
she asked – and locked the cat flap.

Flora calmed down at last. She helped Nana do some mixing and stirring. But Flora could see Rufus through the window.

She thought he looked sad.

Next, Grandpop read Flora her

favourite story. But Rufus was

outside Grandpop's window . . .

Flora thought he sounded lonely.

Then they had a drink and
something to eat, and watched TV.
But Rufus was outside that window
as well . . .

Flora thought he might be hungry too.

Oh no,
it's raining!

Now Flora felt bad. Rufus was

outside because of her!

It's all my fault!

Nana and Grandpop didn't look

very happy either.

Poor Rufus!

'I think he's trying to tell you
something, Flora,' said Grandpop.
'Shall we let him in and find out
what it is?' said Nana.

But Flora was still scared of Rufus.

31

'I've got an idea!' said Grandpop suddenly. He whispered in Nana's ear, and Nana smiled.

Making Friends

'How would you like to play a special game, Flora?' said Nana. 'Now, where did I put those old face paints?'

Flora sat very still while Nana painted her face.

Soon Flora looked exactly like . . .

a cat!

Terrific!

Nana and Grandpop waved their wands . . . and Flora could feel herself changing.

AlakaZOO!
AlakaZAM!

She was a cat!

She walked softly and silently. She stared at Nana and Grandpop with her big eyes.

Nice pussy cat!

Purrrr!

She was following them, and
rubbing against their legs!

So now she knew. Rufus walked

quietly because that's what cats do.

And he stared at her and followed

her about because he liked her!

Nana and Grandpop waved their wands . . . and Flora was herself again.

She went straight to the cat flap and

let Rufus in.

Flora looked into his big green eyes.

They weren't so scary any more.

Flora and Rufus touched noses and
made friends.

Purrr!

And later, when Mum came to
take Flora home . . .

Guess who didn't want to go!